SIT ON TOP

STEPHANIE PERRY MOORE

#5

THE *SWOOP* LIST

SIT ON TOP

STEPHANIE PERRY MOORE

darbycreek

MINNEAPOLIS

YPF
Moore

Darby Creek
A division of Lerner Publishing Group, Inc.
241 First Avenue North
Minneapolis, MN 55401 USA

For reading levels and more information, look up this title at
www.lernerbooks.com.

Cover: © Rauluminate/iStock/Thinkstock (teen girl); © Andrew Marginean/
Dreamstime.com (brick wall); © Andrew Scherbackov/Shutterstock.com
(notebook paper).

Interior: © Andrew Marginean/Dreamstime.com (brick hall background);
© Sam74100/Dreamstime.com, pp. 1, 36, 69; © Luba V Nel/Dreamstime.
com, pp. 9, 43, 76; © iStockphoto.com/kate_sept2004, pp. 16, 49, 83;
© Hemera Technologies/AbleStock.com/Thinkstock, pp. 23, 55, 89;
© Rauluminate/iStock/Thinkstock, pp. 30, 62, 96.

Main body text set in Janson Text LT Std 12/17.5.
Typeface provided by Adobe Systems.

Library of Congress Cataloging-in-Publication Data

Moore, Stephanie Perry.
     Sit on top / by Stephanie Perry Moore.
          pages   cm. — (The Swoop List ; #5)
     Summary: Spurred by another message from Leah and aided by Ms.
  Davis, the Swoop girls try to make the world a better place by sharing their
  stories with a group of promiscuous middle schoolers.
     ISBN 978-1-4677-5808-6 (lib. bdg. : alk. paper)
     ISBN 978-1-4677-6053-9 (pbk. : alk. paper)
     ISBN 978-1-4677-6195-6 (EB pdf)
     [1. Conduct of life—Fiction. 2. Dating (Social customs)—Fiction.
  3. Sex—Fiction. 4. Interpersonal relations—Fiction. 5. High schools—
  Fiction. 6. Schools—Fiction.] I. Title.
  PZ7.M788125Sit 2015
  [Fic]—dc2   2014031436

Manufactured in the United States of America
1 – SB – 12/31/14

For
my violets

Ravin Acree
Bryce Bradley
Emerald Dawson
Gabrielle Fisher
Kaityln Forest
LonDon Levell-Wilkins
Rickayla Mitchell
Sheldyn Moore
Jayla Powell
Ashley Shaw
Sydney Sims
Jordyn Taylor-Utley

You are precious young ladies
sitting on top of life.
I'm so thankful to help you
twirl into brilliance!

CHAPTER ONE

Toughest (Sanaa's Beginning)

As Sanaa Mathis looked at her reflection in the mirror, she had to be honest with herself. Though a girl standing in a gorgeous prom gown was staring back at her, she knew if she did a self-evaluation, she would realize she was still a work in progress. She hated not being as put together as the person she saw in the mirror.

Over the last five months, she'd gone through so much. She and her ex-best friend, Toni, secretly liked the same fine hunk, Miles. Toni had been too shy to talk to Miles for herself, but was bold enough to ask Sanaa to talk to the guy on her behalf. Reluctantly, Sanaa complied, even though she had her own feelings for Miles. When Sanaa finally talked to Miles, he told her he liked her—not her friend. Because she liked him too, they connected. Sanaa had kept it from Toni until it all blew up in her face.

Next thing Sanaa knew, she was named as the first person on the swoop list, a horrible list of girls at her school who were deemed "easy" by whoever wrote the list. She was ridiculed by most people in the school. Four other girls had been named on the swoop list. But out of the madness, all five of the swoop list girls had bonded together. And a melting pot of hope sprung forth.

Now Sanaa was at an after-prom slumber party with the rest of her new friends. She didn't want to take off her gown because she didn't want the fairy tale to end. She was about to graduate, and she had to face the one last thing that was in her way: her ruined relationship with the girl she betrayed. But it wasn't so easy to reconcile with someone who hated your guts, and Sanaa knew it.

Out of nowhere, the toughest swoop list girl,

Willow Dean, appeared and said, "Why do you care about her so much?"

"What? What are you talking about?" Sanaa tried denying.

"I can look at you and see in your eyes that you care. You're thinking about Toni. She isn't your friend."

And as much as Sanaa knew Willow was right and even took the blame for ruining her friendship with Toni, she didn't want it to be true. Sanaa couldn't face Willow. She merely huffed, hoping Willow would let it go.

"Listen to me. She's not your friend," Willow said, pushing her point. "You want a reminder? She's gathered a whole bunch of other girls together to say they want to beat our tails. She showed up to the prom today and tried to convince you she was with your man. Any and everything she can do to get under your skin, she's doing. Screw her."

"Why do you talk so foul?" Sanaa lifted up her head and asked.

Sanaa remembered last month when they were standing in practically this very same spot in Willow's crib, arguing. But this rational, intelligent, brown beauty didn't want to go down that crazy path again. She wanted to get better in life and move forward, not get bitter and move backward.

Being honest, Sanaa took a calmer approach. "You know what, Willow? Let me back up. I know you got my back. I know you care about me. And I know I shouldn't care about Toni, but I can't get her out of my mind."

"And, Willow, you shouldn't ask her to," Olive Bell said in a sleepy voice.

Olive had a lot going on in her life too. Living in a group home and getting caught up with a gang leader was just the start of her issues. Even now she was involved with a guy who lived at the foster home with her. Their relationship was finally getting back on track after her ex, the gang leader Tiger, and Charles, her current beau, had started a feud that escalated to mad violence.

Olive added, "You got to leave her alone, Willow. People want to be true to their hearts, and they want to try to fix things."

Willow looked at Olive and motioned for her to keep it real. "But some stuff you need to leave alone, Olive. Right? It ain't like you trying to reconcile with Tiger and his crazy self."

In a heated tone, Olive lashed back, "No, but honestly, I don't want things to be as volatile as they have been. I've been thinking about how to fix it, and coming up with the right solution is not easy. So I'm just saying, we're Sanaa's girls. Whatever is going on with her, we shouldn't tell her to forget it."

"Thank you!" Sanaa said, walking over to Olive and kissing her on the cheek a few times.

"What are y'all doing up?" said Octavia Streeter, the redheaded, newly crowned prom queen, with her hair all crazed and her crown still on top.

"You're going to break that thing," Willow said, pointing to the mangled crown.

"Yeah, let me get it out of your hair," the lovely, Hispanic Pia Alvarez popped up and said.

Sanaa joked, "Girl don't touch it. I tried to get the bling out of her head earlier tonight, and she wasn't having any of that."

They all laughed. The tension melted. Sanaa exhaled.

"This is how it should be," Sanaa said, feeling good about their connection. "Girls just having fun."

"Yeah, but we're about to go off to college," Pia said.

"Speak for yourself. I'm still trying to figure out what the heck I'm doing," Willow uttered.

"Where is Dawson going to school?" Sanaa teased.

Olive joked, "Yep, because wherever that's going to be, you're probably going too."

"Ha ha, hee hee," Willow fake-laughed. "Of all of us, I'm the last one who's going to be following some boy somewhere. You know I got accepted to Spelman. For real, for real I'm probably headed there. For sure ain't following no dude."

All the rest of them nodded in agreement. Sanaa loved Willow's strength. She just wished her friend wasn't so hard. But dealing with her own flaws, she didn't condemn Willow.

Olive said, "I'm just playing with you, Willow. Ease up."

Willow added, "I know it. I know it. I know it. Just . . . I'm frustrated."

"About what?" Sanaa asked her.

Sensing they wanted her to chill, Willow shared, "I don't know. It's like you guys always want things to be just perfect, and sometimes it's not going to be that way. You can't be all sweet. People will run over you."

Suddenly they heard a bang. All of them huddled together. Willow looked out of her window and saw people egging Sanaa's car.

"What in the world is going on?" Willow yelled.

The girls rushed outside. All of them ran to the left, but Sanaa ran to the right, towards the back of her car, and came face-to-face with Miss Toni. When the getaway car pulled up, the car door opened, Toni dashed inside, and the car took off. Upset, Sanaa reflected that maybe Willow was right. Maybe if you're too sweet and too soft, people will walk all over you. That truly pissed Sanaa off. Her former best friend hated her so much that she was going to damage her property. Why, after all of that, did Sanaa still have such a heart for Toni? She wanted to hold Toni in her heart, but she let her go. That decision was the toughest.

CHAPTER TWO
Craziest (Willow's Beginning)

"I can't believe we let them get away," Willow said. She looked dead in Sanaa's face when all five of the girls got back inside Willow's house after chasing away the culprits who were messing with Sanaa's car.

"I guess my car is too ugly to egg," Octavia tried joking to lighten the mood.

"It's not funny. Nothing's funny about this, Octavia," Willow said. "I knew we should've pounced on them heffas when we had the chance."

"And what would that have solved?" Sanaa uttered in a somber voice.

Willow blasted, "It would've let them know that they can't just show up anytime they want in the wee hours of the night!"

Sanaa screamed, "What? You did almost the same thing to Toni a few weeks back, cutting the fool at two in the morning in her freaking yard!"

Willow was so tired of Sanaa taking up for her friend who betrayed her. Or had Sanaa betrayed Toni? Willow was still confused about how it all went down. The point was that their relationship was irreconcilable, and Sanaa needed to come to terms with that fact.

"You can't be friends with everybody," Willow huffed and said. "And begging criminals is stupid as—"

"Okay, okay, guys. Settle down," Pia said. "The two of y'all gonna fuss at each other again? I won't come over here and spend the night if every time we do, the two of y'all are gonna argue!"

Sanaa said, "I'm not arguing with Willow."

Willow pointed out, "That's right, because you don't argue. Make me the bad one."

"Like I'm the one who made you go over to Toni's house last month and cause a scene?" Sanaa shouted.

Willow stepped up to her and yelled, "To defend your honor, with your ungrateful behind! Plus, I didn't destroy any property. She did!"

"Okay! I just asked y'all to calm down," Pia said, rushing between them with her phone. "Look, this is crazy. You're not gonna believe this. Remember how all y'all got letters from the dead Leah girl? Now I got one. It's another eerie text message. We gotta get to the bottom of this."

Pia showed the message to the other girls.

Dear Swoop List Girls,

Congrats to you girls for holding it together. I see you're making a difference in the lives of young people by passing on your story. That's admirable. But now you're gonna have to dig even deeper and go to a much tougher place. Get ready to execute the final step in making sure that you conquer the swoop list, instead of the swoop list conquering you.

*To truly sit on top, you need to find out
who put you on the swoop list and fix them.
Some of your friends may not be up to the
challenge, but it's the only way to end this
cycle. Trust me.*

Your Angel, Leah

"Okay, this is weird," Sanaa said.

"If she's really telling us to help the people
who hurt us, she is *not* an angel," Willow huffed.

"Yeah, I'm really tired of this too," Olive said.

Pia uttered, "Come on, we promised each
other we were gonna try to figure out who this
Leah girl is. What the heck are we waiting for?"

Sanaa said, "Well, with prom and everything, I guess we just got sidetracked. We're
about to graduate in a little while."

"Don't you guys wanna know who wrote
this?" Pia said.

Everyone nodded except for Willow. Willow
was so done with complying. She wanted the
other girls to get backbones.

Pia went over to Willow, put her arm around
her, and said, "Come on. Live a little. Have a

little adventure. Whoever is writing these notes knows all five of us."

"Remember that we found Leah's obituary? She lived in the city of Warner Robbins. This girl is not alive," Willow said. "I'm not tryna get caught up in who's trifling enough to use her identity. You know what? I'm about to go call my boo."

"Ooh, so you and Dawson cool again?" Olive teased.

"You better see if Charles made it back from prom and is on house arrest again, while you messin' with me," Willow said.

Olive didn't take too kindly to the joke, but Willow was telling the truth. By a judge's order, Charles had to wear an ankle bracelet. He'd gotten it removed to go to prom, but at the end of the night, he'd had to be back at the group home with his ankle bracelet back in place.

Before Willow could exit the room, Sanaa grabbed her arm and said, "Did you have to be rude like that?"

Willow said, "Olive knows I was just playing with her. Quit making a big deal out of nothing.

Besides, you act like you're above everybody, but you sneaky too."

"What are you talking about?"

"What am I talking about? Remember when my car got painted? I think it was Toni and Hillary that did it. And now I saw Toni out there, messing up your car. Hillary was probably driving getaway. You let them go, but I'm not gonna let them get away with this crap. What is wrong with the truth? You're on me because I told Olive she needs to make sure Charles got home in time? If he is late, there are consequences. I just told her to check on him. I wasn't making fun about it. I wasn't saying it's horrible that she's dating a guy with metal around his ankle. I just stated a fact to my friend, being me. But you can't be honest ever. You see a girl you want so badly to be okay with destroying your property, but you let her tail go!"

Sanaa dropped her head and turned around. She started to tear up, but Willow wasn't backing down. Sanaa had pushed her to a place where the real Willow was now loose.

Willow offered, "You need to woman up,

Sanaa, because trying to kiss up to somebody's butt who basically just told you to kiss hers is the craziest."

CHAPTER THREE

Darkest (Olive's Beginning)

On Sunday afternoon, Olive enjoyed sitting with her head nuzzled against Charles's chest. She loved spending time with the swoop list girls, but her heart went pitter-patter when she was with Charles. She couldn't believe that while she'd been looking for love all these years, she'd been actually living in a group home with the guy she'd fall for. Yeah, Olive had caught Charles staring at her every now and then, being a little nervous around her, and maybe overly so. Maybe she should have picked up on it. But she couldn't go back and change how long it took for her to find him. She was just grateful that things were perfect now.

"You took me to the prom," Olive said.

"Sorry I gave you such a hard time about it. You looked beautiful, too."

"And you were quite dapper in a tux."

"What you trying to say? Ya boy can't clean up?"

"Oh, I know you can clean up." She seductively smiled his way.

"I thought you were coming back here after the prom," Charles said. "But I should have known you wanted to hang with yo' girls."

"If you wanted to hang, you should have said so."

"It was cool. I was happy seeing y'all dancing. Had all us dudes just standing around, admiring the view. But I've been longing to do this," he said as his hands roamed everywhere on her frame, and he kissed her.

"Oh my gosh, what are you doing?"

"Trying to take my mind off of stuff."

She pulled back. "You stressin'? Then let's talk. You know I care."

"I don't know if I'm the right guy for you."

"What are you talking about? Didn't you just feel the attraction between the two of us?" Olive asked.

"Ms. B was telling me about all the scholarship offers you got," Charles said. Since Ms. B ran the group home Charles and Olive lived in, she was involved in helping them plan for what was next. "She said your caseworker planned to help you narrow down a scholarship option. You'll be going to college in a few months."

"And, so . . . come with me. You got selected to apply for some scholarships too."

"I know, but I'm right at a 2.9. I'm probably not going to get a 3.0. I'm not going to be able to afford college."

"With grant and aid, you'll be able to go," Olive insisted.

"It's not for me right now. I need a little bit more discipline in my life. Plus, if I go to the military, I can get some of it paid for. The government has been taking care of me all my life, and I'm a little tired of that."

Olive replied, "But that's what it's there for . . . people like us."

"Why should the state have to take care of me because my parents were trifling? I want to earn my own way. And to me, a man who deserves you should want to do that . . . legitimately, not like crazy Tiger."

Olive hated that Tiger's name was brought up between the two of them. She knew it was a sore spot. She looked away.

"You disappointed in me?" Charles asked.

"No, you go to the military. I'll support that."

"If I go to the military, I don't think the two of us can be together. It will just be unrealistic for me to ask you to not look at all those college boys."

"Then I'll go to the military too."

But Charles just shook his head. "Who's to say we'll be stationed in the same places? That makes no type of sense, Olive. You shouldn't hold yourself back because I didn't do what I needed to do in high school."

"But what about us?" Olive said as she brushed his cheek with the back of her hand and gazed into his eyes. "Don't you want to stay together? You're avoiding the question."

Charles changed the subject. "What did you girls talk about last night at your slumber thing?"

"You guys." She giggled.

"Yeah, I guess I should have figured that. Is that all y'all do? Sit around and gossip?"

"No, no, actually . . . it got interesting. Toni and probably Hillary and some of the other petty girls at the school came over in the wee hours of the morning and egged Sanaa's car. Of course, Willow was super pissed. And supposedly Willow's car got painted earlier in the year, so she's out for blood."

"You guys gossiped and talked about more fighting?"

"No. We also discussed the swoop list. There's a lot to it, but long story short, we're all trying to figure out who put us on it."

He frowned. "Why would you have to figure it out? You know who it was."

"No, I don't," Olive said with a real attitude.

"Yes, you do. It was Tiger."

"It was not Tiger. Why would he put me on the list?"

"Why did he do a bunch of the things he

did to you? I can't believe that you would even question it."

"You don't need to be jealous of him anymore. Let go of the whole Tiger animosity thing. He would have nothing to gain by hurting me that way. At the time, I was his girl."

Upset, Charles lashed out. "You seem like you might still need to be his girl . . . defending his behind. You talking about how I need to get over him . . . looks like you're the one who needs to get over him."

Charles moved Olive off of him. He got up and paced the floor. She placed her hands on her head.

Charles ranted, "Here I am, stressed out about wanting to figure out a future with you, and it still seems like you're thinking about a future with somebody else."

"Oh my gosh, you're a jerk," Olive said as she took a nearby pillow from the couch and chucked it his way.

Olive desperately wanted to talk through the discord, but Charles wasn't interested. He turned and headed out the door. As soon as he was gone and she was sitting there all alone, she knew that their relationship was at its darkest.

CHAPTER FOUR
Brightest (Octavia's Beginning)

"I can't believe you got me out here fishing," Octavia said to Shawn, her boyfriend, as she jabbed him in the side with one arm and struggled to hold her pole with the other.

"You ain't even doin' it right. You the one who wanted to come out here, giving me a hard time about hanging out with your dad all the time, and now you don't wanna fish!" he teased her back.

"I know, I just wanted to spend some fun time with you," she said as the sun beamed down brightly on her. "I can't believe we're about to graduate! This is crazy!"

"Yeah, and I don't wanna think about nothing right now but you."

"But I'm a muddy, stinky mess," she said as he leaned her backwards.

"And sexy," he said as he crawled on top of her.

Although they were in a compromising position, they kept things on the up and up. They teased and bit each other's ears. They were slobbering as they gave a few pecks on the lips. All clothes stayed on, and no body parts were shared.

Looking up at the blazing sun, Octavia reflected. "I've got to do something with my life so that I can be successful one day. I mean, my dad has had to do a lot on his own, and it's not like we live in the best part of town. My car looks like it's gonna fall apart. My poor clothes need updating. We can't afford that. I hate that I'm sitting here complaining. It could be worse. I think about Olive all the time, and you, and I don't know. Am I weirding you out talking about this?"

"No. I don't need you to take pity on me,

and I'm sure Olive doesn't want you to take pity on her either. Our life is our life. We're comfortable with who we are, but you got a point. We want more for ourselves, and that's probably why I feel like a failure."

"What are you talking about? We're about to graduate. We're in the prime of our lives."

"Yeah, but everybody's talking about what's next—college, a job, the military. I don't wanna go into the military like Charles, and I'm not ready for college either. It's not like I wanna sit on my butt and do nothing, but I don't want a minimum-wage job. I don't know. Honestly, if I had another year of high school, I'd be alright with it. Freshmen, sophomores, and juniors just don't even know how good they got it. This facing the real world thing is no joke." And on that comment, he sat up and threw his line back into the water.

She looked over at him and hated that she couldn't think of what to say to encourage him about what was next. She knew she had to give some hard thought to it. She'd been so consumed with her own life that she hadn't spent much time reflecting on what was next for Shawn. One thing she knew was that he had a bright future. He needed to believe that. But at least he was being real about what was on his mind.

Octavia wasn't being so forthcoming. She'd just left the fun slumber party gone south with the swoop list girls. Octavia shut down after they read the letter from Leah. The letter had challenged the girls to find out who put them on the swoop list and deal with that person. How was Octavia going to tell her girls that she put herself on the list? Octavia had already told Shawn and the school counselor, Ms. Davis. But telling her friends was much more difficult. Once they knew the truth, how could they ever care about her again? How could she face graduation isolated from them? In Octavia's mind, that was the only outcome she could see if she told them everything.

"Gosh, I must not be the only one with something on my mind. It's been fifteen minutes, and you've been quiet. What's wrong? I didn't mean to bring you out here to depress you," Shawn uttered in a caring way.

"There are no answers to my problems. But I have been thinking about yours."

"What do you mean?"

"The technical school."

"What am I good at?"

"I don't know, but there're lots of trades—automotive, plumbing, culinary."

"Wait, don't sleep. I do love to cook," Shawn joked.

"Okay. Well, maybe we should pursue it."

"They have a school for that? Like, one you don't have to go to college for?" Shawn asked hopefully.

"From what I've seen, some colleges do have a culinary degree. But there are technical schools that you can go to just learn how to cook, and it's not a four-year school. You'd come out and be some kind of chef."

"I need to look into that. 'Cause sometimes when I'm sitting at home with Ms. B and she flips to the cooking channels, I stay and watch with her. I get mesmerized and try to make the dishes. Before I got shot, I cooked for the house many days. I pride myself on how I chop my food. I put in other ingredients so it tastes really good. I don't know, cooking school...you might be on to something," Shawn said with hope rising.

"Look at you! Okay, okay. See, you're smiling."

"Now let me help you out. What's up? You still worried about telling your friends that you put yourself on the swoop list? Or you did tell them last night, and they're mad at you? Talk to me. Be real."

"You think you know me well," Octavia said, hating to broach the subject. "I haven't told them, but I really want to. They're my best friends. I mean, after you of course."

"Oh, yeah, yeah, yeah," Shawn played with her and said. "After me of course."

"You're silly, Shawn." She lifted her hand from the rod to hit him, but when she pulled up she felt a little tugging.

"You caught something!" he said, helping her reel in the line.

It was the cutest little four-inch fish. They both laughed. Octavia was proud, though. It was her first time fishing, and she caught a fish. She was ecstatic.

Octavia smiled. "Can't wait to tell Daddy I caught something."

"That's right. You put your all into it, and something came back to you. So trust that with your friends. Share from the heart. Put it all out there. You'll be satisfied with the results."

Throwing the little minnow back, she said, "Look at you, making me feel like my future with them is the brightest."

CHAPTER FIVE
Steepest (Pia's Beginning)

Jackson High was all abuzz as Kenny, Isaiah, and Sebastian were ushered off the premises in handcuffs. Since it happened before the first bell rang, a crowd of students and teachers watched the drama unfold.

Pia also had a front-row seat. Most of the school knew that Pia had been a victim of rape. Rumors had been flying for weeks. The police had told Pia that she didn't have to be in school during the arrests. But she'd decided that she wanted to be there. She wasn't gloating. She wasn't happy this was happening. It actually brought back memories of the horrifying things that the three young men had done to her back in December. As much as Pia wanted to block memories of the rape from her mind, she was emotionally scarred from their actions. She had become pregnant through the rape and then had an abortion. Recalling that procedure was painful for Pia too.

Since Pia was a caring person, she didn't want to harbor hatred in her heart. But some of her classmates rolled their eyes at her and called her names as the police left with the boys, Seeing this, Pia was beyond angry. The boys had violated her, and yet people were supporting them. Pia wondered why she had no support.

"I can't believe this! Those idiots took everything from me! Why are folks mad at me? This is so wrong!" Pia cried out.

Before more horrible accusations could be thrown her way, her boyfriend, Stephen, rushed over to her from out of the crowd. He grabbed her hand and pulled her to an isolated corner. Tears flowed from her eyes, and he held her, wanting to take away her pain.

"You can't worry about those people. Who

cares what they think? Don't let them get to you."

She replied, "But now they aren't going to be able to march with our class at graduation because of the pending charges and stuff. Should I have looked the other way after all they did to me? Should I have not cared? Come on, Stephen. Why do I feel like the villain when they were the ones who were monsters?"

"I'm telling you, you shouldn't feel that way. Don't stress. Don't let it get to you. Come here. Let me take your mind off of it," he said as he pulled her close and kissed her.

"This is just sick," a voice said.

The loud voice startled Pia and Stephen. They backed apart. Neither were pleased to see Hillary standing there with her hands on her hips. Hillary was always talking smack about the swoop list girls.

Pia looked at her and said, "What's your problem?"

Hillary scoffed, "You are my problem, sitting here all cuddled up with him like the world is okay when you done messed up the lives of the best ballers we got."

"You need to keep it moving," Stephen said to Hillary, letting her know that her jab to him not being one of the best ballers didn't faze him.

"Don't tell me what to do, tattletale," Hillary replied as she got all up in his face.

Stephen grunted, "You know what. I'm not even going to let you affect me."

"You're just a punk. Anybody who's going to tell on his teammates better be watching his back around here," Hillary said as she shoved him.

Stephen went to sock her. The last thing Pia wanted was for Stephen to have more trouble because of her. She motioned for him to settle down.

Hillary didn't let up. "You need to slow your roll. You don't want me to tell everything I know."

"What you gon' tell?" Stephen said, blowing her off.

Confidently working her neck, Hillary responded, "Don't make me go there. That's all I'm saying."

Frowning, Stephen said, "You ain't got nothing to tell on me."

"What she talking about?" Pia asked.

He said, "I don't know. She's just trying to make trouble. Ignore her."

"Oh, I'm not trying to make trouble. But it will be trouble if I tell it," Hillary smiled and reported.

"What you going to say? I wanted to be with you one day? In your dreams," Stephen joked.

Hillary said, "Oh no, I know you didn't want a sweet girl like me. You wanted to be with a ho."

"What you talking about?" Stephen asked.

"Tell your little girlfriend who put her on the swoop list," Hillary demanded, looking like she knew Pia was going to hate the answer.

Stephen's yellow skin turned red. Pia looked at him with desperation in her eyes. She was basically pleading for Hillary's words not to have merit. But Stephen said nothing.

"Oh my gosh. You put me on the swoop list? Wait a minute, all this time you been after me, and you put me on the swoop list? You been acting like you cared, and you put me on the swoop list! Say something!" Pia yelled out as she pounded on his chest.

"It's not like that. You don't understand," Stephen pitifully tried to explain.

Hillary grinned and grunted, "Oh, it's just like that. And I know he put you on there."

"How do you know?" Pia grabbed Hillary's shirt.

Moving Pia's hands away, Hillary boasted, "Because I am the author of the swoop list. Booyah! I put you on it after he sent your information to me. He said you were too fast, and now he can't wait to keep all the guys off you so he can get with you. Have you hit it yet, Stephen? Making her think you really care when you hurt her so bad."

Pia was devastated at that moment. For a split second, she wished she had a knife so she could stab both of them. She didn't know what she was more shocked about, who the author of the whole entire swoop list was or who the one who put her on it was. Both were horrifying, so she ran away. She'd been through a lot over the past few months, but now her depression was at its steepest.

CHAPTER SIX
Truest (Sanaa's Middle)

Sanaa was feeling good, and she had true pep in her step. Graduation was only two weeks away, and although it still hurt that she and Toni would probably never reconcile, she was thankful for what she did have: four other good friends. Although she knew friendships with girls weren't easy, she was determined to make it work. So when she saw Pia headed toward her in tears, she stopped her.

"Okay, wait a minute. You're a basket case, like you're one of these seniors around here who just got notice that they not gon' graduate. I know that's not your story. Tell me what is wrong," Sanaa said.

Shaking and with red eyes, Pia replied, "I'm not in the mood to talk right now, so just let me go."

"No, I'm your girl. I'm not going anywhere. Talk to me! If you can't be real with me, what good is friendship? Pia, tell me, what's wrong?"

When Pia felt Sanaa's sincerity, she said, "I just found out who wrote the swoop list. Also, I learned who put me on the list. With those two things, what could be right?"

Sanaa didn't know how to respond to that. All five of them had made a pact to find out who put them on the list. On the surface, she still wanted to find out. However, deep down, Sanaa was so happy about graduation and didn't want to do anything to ruin that feeling. Sanaa rationalized that if Pia was this upset over what she'd found out, prying into her own painful truth would only bring misery.

Putting aside her own dilemma of who put her on the list, Sanaa tended to her girl. "So, who was it?"

"Who was who? Who wrote the swoop list,

or who put me on the swoop list?" Pia said with blazing eyes.

"Is it the same person?"

Pia shook her head.

"Okay, so you gon' make me guess? Is it one of them freaks who got carted out of here not too long ago?" Pia looked away, and Sanaa continued, "Don't feel bad for them. I hate seeing anybody our age in trouble with the law too, but after what those three did to you, I know they are capable of anything. Putting you on the swoop list. Stupid thing. Jerks."

Pia shook her head more and said, "You'd think the person who created the Jackson High swoop list would be a guy. I mean, what girl in her right mind would sell out other girls, right?"

Sanaa clutched her heart, "Oh, for real, is it Willow's nemesis?"

"Yep, that Hillary witch is behind the whole swoop list. At first I didn't know which betrayal made me feel worse, you know? I do feel bad knowing that Hillary betrayed all of us females. But what really hurts the worst is knowing the one who's been kissing up behind me like he really cares about me gave her my name!"

"What are you talking about?" Sanaa asked.

"I'm saying Stephen put me on the list. I was just about to let my guard down and put my tongue in his mouth when Hillary comes over and makes it clear that all that glitters ain't gold. Boy, was she right. He was so fake. How could he hurt me like that, Sanaa?"

Giving her girl a hug, Sanaa said, "I would have never even suspected him."

"Me either. How dumb am I?"

"Can I talk to you, please?" Stephen asked, startling both of them.

Pia turned around and slapped him hard. She dashed off. Sanaa was boiling hot.

"Oh my gosh, Stephen! You put her on the list?" Sanaa said.

He shared, "She won't listen to me, but I need you to."

Sanaa just put up her hand and walked away. She didn't want to hear any words from Stephen. She was in shock that a guy close to her girl would sell her out for any reason.

"Hey, you wanna wait up for me or what?" Miles asked her.

Sanaa had seen Miles standing close to Stephen before he caught up to her. Sanaa and Miles had been dating on and off for a few months.

"Miles, were you walking with Stephen?" she asked.

"Yeah, he told me what happened. You should hear him out," Miles said.

"You know what he did, and you were still walking with him, and now you're defending him?"

He touched her arm. "Look, I don't even know Stephen like that. The cat was just asking for some advice, and his rationale for what he did sounded cool to me. But I don't wanna have any beef with you because of what's going on with somebody else's relationship."

She jerked away. "Oh, so, did you put me on the list, and you think you got a rationale too to explain it all away?"

"What you talkin' about?" he said as he stopped her in her tracks. "Wait, wait, wait. Come here. Look at me. I didn't sell you out.

Tell me you believe I didn't put you on the list. You asked me that months ago. I told you then I didn't do it, and I'm standing by it now. I didn't do it! Both of us know who put you on the list."

"Now hearing that a girl wrote it, and Toni's been all cool with Hillary, I guess I do know for sure who lied on me and ruined my rep."

"Wait, Hillary wrote the list?" Miles questioned.

"You didn't know that?"

"No. I didn't submit nothing to no list. I mean, I heard everything was anonymous about it. But maybe Toni knew Hillary wrote it. I don't know, and I can't say for sure Toni put you on the list, but you were the first girl on the list, and Willow was the second. Suspect," Miles said, making sense to Sanaa.

"I bet you those two heffas planned this mess all the time, and then just got some other stupid guys, like Stephen, to go along adding other girls' names to it. But them two would've been satisfied if it was just Willow and me on the list. Oh my gosh, this is so trifling!" Sanaa screamed.

"So you don't think I did it? You truly get me now? I wouldn't sell you out like that. I care about my girl too much to go down that road," Miles slid closer and asked.

"Yes, yes, yes."

"Alright. 'Cause, I'm just sayin' . . . when we first got together an' you told me to keep it secret from Toni, I had your back then too."

"Well, I was wrong about that. Of course we should've told her. I didn't know it'd blow up this bad. Point learned . . . don't keep secrets from your best friend." Sanaa stroked his cheek. "I'm sorry for accusing you. You wouldn't sell me out like that. And I know you're saying you respect my wishes to slow things down."

Eyeing her whole body and licking his lips, Miles said, "When you gon' be ready again?"

"When you put a ring on it!" Sanaa said to him. "But for real, for real, you're there for me as a boyfriend. I know you wouldn't sell me out. You're the truest."

CHAPTER SEVEN

Boldest (Willow's Middle)

"All I know is, I'm going to need my momma to give me my car back," Willow boldly said to Olive as the two of them walked to their respective classes.

"All I know is if you ask her like that, don't hold your breath. Good ol' pastor needs respect," Olive teased.

"Right, right, right. You know I've been begging, being a good girl. But shucks, Olive, it's been months since the car accident that I didn't even cause."

"Yeah, your brother was the one driving, right? And you took the blame for him?"

"Yep. But he actually told my parents last month that is was him driving."

"Really?"

Willow nodded. "I like the knucklehead now. Since I'm getting to leave for college, I'm going to miss him. I told him not to say nothing. They already mad at me. No need for them to be mad at the both of us. He thought that telling would make them give me my car back, but they were just mad that I lied, so they kept my car anyway. It's graduation time, and I want my wheels. I'm tired of depending on other people. I'm about to text her right now."

"You better be sweet about it."

Willow texted, "Give me my dang wheels, shoot!" But before she sent it, she looked over at Olive, who was reading the text and shaking her head. Willow erased it, nodded in agreement that she needed to back off, and typed, "Mom, I love you. I'm sorry I was protecting my little brother. Please, if you can find it in your heart to forgive me, I'd love to drive the next couple weeks. Can I have my keys when I get home today and go somewhere with my girls?"

Both of them held their breath as they saw three dots scrolling across the bottom of the phone screen, indicating that her mother saw the message and was typing something back. And they never screamed so loud when they saw three letters pop back: "y-e-s."

"What we gonna do? Where we gonna go? I ain't mad at Octavia, but her car put-puts around, and I ain't got no problem with Sanaa's, but it's all vandalized . . . If I see that daggone Hillary . . ."

"There they go right there," Olive said, wishing she could take the words back as she grabbed Willow's arm to stop her from dashing over to Hillary and Toni. "No! Don't go over there."

Willow tugged away and uttered, "Girl, let me go. I'm sick of this heifer. I'm about to show her ain't nobody no punk."

"Wait, let's talk about where we're going later," Olive replied, wanting to distract Willow.

"I don't care. Wherever you want to go," Willow shared, just trying to get to Hillary.

Bright-eyed, Olive lit up. "You mean that? Like, you're not going to take it back? Like, if

I give you some gas money, wherever I want to go, you'll go?"

Willow frowned and asked Olive, "What you talking about doing? You saying it all like that, now I know wherever you're saying I'm not going to want to go. Tell me, Olive. What are you thinking?"

"We need to go to Warner Robbins. I know the name of Leah's school, got directions to where it is. We need to check out this girl who's been sending us letters from beyond the grave and end the whole mystery thing."

"What? Because you don't really believe she could be sending us letters?"

"Of course I don't believe she's actually writing them. She's dead. But let's find out who her friends were. Let's find out who knew her that might know us. Let's do some investigations and put this whole thing to bed."

"Urgh, I'll think about it. They're about to walk away," Willow grunted, seeing Hillary and Toni head off. "I need to talk to this girl right now."

"Well, look who the midnight has dragged

out," Hillary called as Willow sashayed right up to her and stood between her and Toni.

With a rolling neck, Willow yelled, "I don't know what y'all think. Y'all can just get away with anything you want to do, coming to people's houses egging cars and stuff, throwing paint on cars, but I saw you, Hillary."

"You ain't seen nobody," Hillary scoffed back.

Willow stepped closer. "I saw you."

"Show me the proof. We got proof when you went to Toni's house late in the night. Everybody saw you acting stupid in her driveway, but if you saw me . . . show me. Because you must of not talked to your girl if that's all you got beef with me for. I don't have any problems admitting to what I do, boo," Hillary jumped and said to Willow.

"I ain't your boo," Willow said. "And what are you talking about? What did you admit to?"

"You better talk to Pia."

"I'm talking to you!"

"And I said I ain't tellin' ya. Now what?" Hillary said, getting real loud.

Willow was fuming. "You're just a jealous

wench. Always wish you could dance better than me. The only way to get rid of me was to throw me off the dance team. It's not like you got skills of your own that could take me. You wanted all eyes on you when we hit the court, but they weren't, they were on me. And that's been eating you alive."

Hillary shouted, "They were looking at a freak, and once they found that out, they didn't want to look at you no more! You were nasty, opening up your legs for any Tom or Harry. You know how to work your body all right. I feel sorry for those so-called friends of yours because you're the only one who truly deserves to be on the swoop list. How many guys you've been with, Willow? Too many to count? You need to go and get checked to make sure you ain't got VD."

Willow raised her hand and was about to slap Hillary, but Hillary caught her wrist before she could. Willow's eyes watered and her beautiful, dark skin trembled. The heart of the lion was more like a cub.

"What? The truth hurts?" Hillary taunted. "Or now you're just mad that my insults hold truth and are the coldest and boldest?"

CHAPTER EIGHT

Meanest (Olive's Middle)

Olive was thrilled to pieces that she was in Willow's car with the other swoop list girls. They were heading to Warner Robbins High School, Leah's old school. All of the girls agreed that they wanted to figure out the Leah mystery, but no one was really pushing to make it happen. Pia had been helping Olive, but then all of a sudden she mellowed out. Willow was still pissed about being embarrassed by Hillary at the school, and Sanaa and Octavia were just quiet.

Olive said to Willow, "You can't let folks get to you."

"You can't tell me how to feel, Olive. I mean, I know that you're trying to be sweet and helpful and all, but I'm sick and tired of being called a slut. Particularly when the shoe fits."

"Hillary is just a mean girl. Just don't let her ruin you and make you . . ." Olive didn't know how to finish the sentence without hurting Willow's feelings.

"What? Make me mean again too?" Willow asked.

"Yes," Olive uttered. "You've come such a long way. We're getting along so well."

"What was Hillary talking about anyway, Pia?" Willow questioned. "She said you had information about her, or something."

"Well, Sanaa already knows, but y'all aren't going to believe this," Pia said.

"With Hillary, I believe anything. What did she do now?" Willow asked.

Sitting in the front passenger's seat, Sanaa turned around to Pia, who was sitting in the middle, and shook her head like, *Please don't tell her. She doesn't need to hear anything else that's going to set her off with Hillary. She might turn the car around and go fight the girl right now. No, don't say anything!*

"Don't tell her not to tell me," Willow said to Sanaa.

"She needs to know this," Pia replied, tapping Sanaa on the shoulders.

"Well, tell me!" Willow shouted at Pia.

Pia complied and blurted out, "Hillary started the swoop list."

Willow almost wrecked the car. "What? Then she put me on it!"

Olive put her hand on Willow's shoulder. "We all got put on the list, so the fact that a jealous girl put you on there should make you feel better."

"The only thing that's gonna make me feel better is when I whoop her tail. How about that?" Willow said, trying to act tough, but shaking from the emotion.

Trying to keep them all focused, Olive said, "Alright, well, can we just put it all aside for now? Ain't nothing we can do. The school is right up here, and the guidance counselor is waiting to meet us."

Twenty minutes later they were sitting in a conference room in the counselor's office. Olive tried to keep her crew engaged. It was difficult because they all seemed preoccupied.

"Are you Dr. Speed?" Olive said to the older lady with glasses. "Thank you for taking time to meet with us."

"Well, when you called, I had to stay around to make time to speak to you. First, I hate to hear that there's a swoop list out at your school too. One was released at our school with just one name on it. It did such damage. But I don't think we'll ever have another swoop list again."

"That's a great thing," Olive said.

Dr. Speed nodded, but responded, "The problem is it did so *much* damage. So if there's anything I can do to help you all, I'm certainly willing to do it."

Olive looked at her friends and clearly saw their interest waning. She got to the point. "We just wanna know about the girl, Leah Golf—the one name that was on the list. She's been writing us."

"You said that, but you know she's deceased, right?" Dr. Speed questioned.

"Yeah, I keep telling them that it ain't her. I mean, she's not even alive," Willow said.

"Right, but she's written all five of us. She texted some of us from a blocked number. And she's even said in her letters that she's dead. To me it doesn't make sense. We're just here with hope you can shed some light on it," Sanaa explained.

"What happened to her?" Pia asked.

"I'm sure y'all know from when the list came out for your school, it was devastating. Everybody hates you. It's like you're really being bullied. You guys at least had each other to lean on. Imagine if you were the only one all the daggers were pointing toward."

"But what happened to her?" Octavia said.

Olive was happy they were all listening. They needed closure. She just hoped Dr. Speed could give it to them.

Dr. Speed leaned forward and said, "She couldn't take the pressure. Some guys had taken some nude photos of her, and those started surfacing. Things were happening here that we didn't really know about until after she was gone. Everybody felt remorseful after this girl couldn't take it and took her own life. I don't know who's writing you the letters. I know it's not Leah, but her death affected everyone, including me. I wish I would've done more. So, the letter writer could be anyone who knew her, trying to right his or her own personal wrong they did to her. I know that doesn't give you any answers, but if anything in those letters has helped you become stronger, then Leah's death isn't in vain. One thing everybody learned here was that we all looked down on Leah because of this list, and we were wrong to do that. A lot of the rumors about her were proven to be true, but who was anybody to judge? Leah ended her life because, collectively, we were the meanest."

CHAPTER NINE

Deepest (Octavia's Middle)

On the ride back from Warner Robbins, all the girls were somber. Octavia knew everyone felt bad hearing how Leah was tormented at her school in such a bad way that made her take her own life. That in and of itself was depressing.

Adding to the heavyheartedness for Octavia was the fact that she had an extra piece of anxiety weighing on her. She had no idea how she was going to break the truth to the girls she'd grown to love so deeply. Pretending she wasn't holding anything back from them was no longer an option.

"We can't just stay out, y'all," Olive said. "I wanted us to come down here and find out all we could about Leah."

"We didn't find out anything," Willow said.

"Yeah, we found out a lot," Olive defended.

"We found out it could be almost anybody in the school," Sanaa uttered. "Pia, what you think?"

Pia said, "I agree with y'all. I mean, Olive, it's good we went down there, we found out it was truly a girl who went through so much, but we don't know any more than we did before."

"Yes we do. We know that all she went through hurt her so bad that we would never want to be that cruel to anybody, ya know? Aren't we all different from hearing her story? Octavia, what about you?" Olive asked.

The last thing Octavia wanted to do was talk. It was becoming harder and harder for her to live with her own lie. The only thing she wanted to say to any of them were words she knew would make them never speak to her again. However, how could she say those words when they would make her end up just how she started . . . alone?

"What's wrong with you?" Willow looked back and asked Octavia.

Octavia shrugged her shoulders, and that made Olive say, "Yeah, you've been real quiet."

"Everybody's been quiet," Octavia snapped.

"Okay, I'm sorry!" Olive said. "Dang, excuse me."

"I'm hungry," Pia uttered, diminishing the tension.

Thinking she needed to find a way to work things out, Octavia said, "Why don't you guys come over to my house? I can fix us some spaghetti."

"What? You're Italian now?" Willow joked.

"Ha, ha, ha. You hungry or not?" Octavia asked with a little sass.

She knew she was going to need it because if they agreed, she had made up in her mind that she was not going to let them leave without being transparent. Her moment of truth was here. She would not let the sun set without them knowing.

About an hour later, they were all sitting around Octavia's dinner table. There were only four chairs, but she was happy to play hostess and let them all be comfortable. She knew what she was going to share would be anything but comfortable.

"You can sit down with me," Sanaa said, being so caring.

"Girl, maybe you are a little Italian," Willow messed with her. "This spaghetti is the bomb."

"You're just hungry," Olive said as Pia laughed.

Pia clutched her heart and stopped laughing. "See, I'm not even supposed to be happy right now."

"Yeah, so tell us about this. Stephen put you on the list?" Willow questioned, wanting confirmation. Pia nodded. "That is so trifling! I hope you're through with that. No matter what he comes back and tries to say, Pia, you're done, over, and finished with his behind. Right?"

"For sure!" Pia quickly responded.

"Yeah, that's what's up," Willow said to her.

Octavia was hearing all of the commotion, all of the talking, all of the playful jibber-jabber, but she was wasting time. She knew they were finishing their meal. She knew she needed to get to it.

Octavia hit the table and said, "I need to talk to y'all."

"Okay, you don't have to be so violent," Willow uttered.

Octavia softened and said, "I didn't mean to startle you all, but I know who put me on the list."

"Urgh, right! And if Stephen put Pia on the list, please don't tell me Shawn did the same thing to you," Willow accused.

"No!" Olive shouted. "Shawn wouldn't put her on the list. Besides, it wasn't Shawn, 'cause I bet it was that other white girl who walks around the school that nobody talks to. She's jealous of you, Octavia. That's who did it!"

"Do we have another white girl at the school?" Sanaa joked as they all giggled a quick bit. "It might have been a teacher. You know some of them are haters too."

"It could be a girl," Pia said. "A girl started the list with another girl, so won't nothing shock me no more."

Octavia couldn't take them getting so angry at the wrong folks. Finally she said, "I put myself on the list, okay!"

"What you mean, you put yourself on the list?" Willow asked boldly in an angry tone.

"I put myself on the list," Octavia repeated.

Sanaa said, "Wait, hold up. You been acting like you were a victim, and this whole time it's been like a joke, like a game? You been playing us?"

"No, no, no, it was nothing like that," Octavia pleaded.

"Well, what was it like?" Olive said, completely upset. "We've been confiding in you, like you understood what we were going through, and you put yourself on the list? How could you do that to us?"

"Come on, y'all, we out," Willow said.

"Please, let me explain! Please, let me talk!" Octavia cried out.

"Are you kidding? What else do you have to say?" Willow told her.

Octavia knew she couldn't make them hear her out, and as Willow pointed out, what else was there to say? She did it for a lame reason, and all this time she'd never told them, and that was bad. Octavia made a plea to each of them individually. When they all vanished, basically saying they never wanted to see her again, she fell to the floor and wallowed, knowing that the girls she had come to care about the most, she had now hurt the deepest.

CHAPTER TEN

Oddest (Pia's Middle)

"White girls. All this time she was lying to us. Would do anything to put herself in the good graces of the popular kids. Just makes me sick," Willow said in an angry tone to Pia, Sanaa, and Olive as she drove them away from Octavia's home, really pissed at her.

Olive joined in the bashing and said, "I just can't believe I fell for her bull, tryna act like she was one of us all along when she was nowhere near one of us. And wait until Shawn finds out. He thinks she's so sweet and innocent."

"She's anything but," Sanaa added.

Pia wasn't adding to the conversation. She

was actually pretty salty that the three of them were so mad. Yeah, she was disappointed to learn that Octavia had duped them, but there had to be some reason. And to bring up the whole white girl thing pissed Pia off to no end. Did they talk about her race or color when she wasn't around too? Were they truly swoop list sisters or not? The love didn't seem to be unconditional, and that bothered Pia a lot. But what also bothered her was that her phone kept blowing up. She looked down and sighed, seeing Stephen text her yet again.

"When will you get the point?" she screamed.

"You want to tell Octavia off too? Let it out, girl," Willow said.

Pia shouted, "No, but I wanna tell you off."

"Excuse me?" Willow said, about to swerve all over the road, looking back at Pia.

Pia explained, "I'm just sayin'. You were pretty harsh on Octavia. We didn't even give her a chance to explain." All three of them looked at her like she had lost her mind and needed to be in an insane asylum, wrapped in a white coat that buckled in the back. "I'm not crazy. We're supposed to be friends. Good friends, the best of friends. Where's the grace? We can't turn on each other."

Olive said, "Yeah, we are supposed to have a real friendship based on truth."

"Forget all of that politically correct stuff. Let's cut to the chase. You mad because I said she pulled some white girl junk, huh?" Willow chimed in, grunting and on point.

"Well, I didn't like what she did," Pia said to Willow.

"It's true. She did pull some ditzy white girl junk," Willow insisted. "Ain't nobody tryna feel sorry for her either. Octavia might be a minority at this school, but we're the real minorities in life. Olive, with her multiracial behind, you with your Hispanic self, and me and Sanaa... chocolate beauties. We all might look like a million bucks, but we're double minorities, women of color. Octavia ain't gonna have our same struggle, with her red-haired self."

"I mean, why's it always gotta be about color, though? We're past all of that," Pia defended.

"We ain't past nothing," Willow boldly

responded before popping Sanaa in the passenger seat to get her to speak up.

Sanaa sat up and grabbed her arm. "Naw, Pia's got a point, Willow. Speak for yourself."

"'Cause, Willow, you ain't speaking for me," Olive said.

"Oh, I know you don't think because you half white, you white?" Willow asked her.

Rolling her eyes in the rearview mirror so Willow could see her reaction, Olive declared, "No, I don't."

Willow scoffed, "Because I'm just sayin'."

Olive said, "No, I clearly know I'm black. When you got a little chocolate mixed in the milk, light chocolate, dark chocolate, it ain't pure milk no more. You ain't gotta tell me. But, Shawn's my brother, and he's white as snow. Pia, it's not about color for me. It's the fact that Octavia lied."

"I agree with her," Sanaa said. "Her color ain't got nothing to do with it. I'd be equally upset if I found out one of you guys did the same thing. I just don't know why she'd do that, and I don't have time to sit there and tell her how to treat the people she's supposed to care about."

Pia added, "But isn't that just funny, because you didn't tell everything to the one person who was supposed to be your best friend. You claim you had a good reason, and even still to this day you want Toni to forgive you."

"Ooh, she got you on that!" Willow laughed. "But forget what y'all say. I'm still mad at that white heffa."

Pia shook her head and sighed. Pia had shut Sanaa up. Now she knew she needed to work on the other two.

Pia looked beside her and said, "And Olive, you were down when Charles was mad because you went to the judge behind his back. You thought if he'd just listen to you, he'd give you a chance to show how much you care and forgive you. And ultimately, when he opened up his mind, he did. How can you not give Octavia the same chance? And Willow—"

"What?" Willow screamed.

Pia got loud back and said, "So many people sent a petition around to kick you out of school.

You were mad at us because we didn't tell you about it. But we didn't wanna hurt your feelings. Once you found out why we didn't tell you, you forgave us and realized that we had your back all the time. And remember how you misled your parents and made them think your brother was the one who had the car accident, all because you wanted to protect him?"

"So what you sayin', the redhead wanted to protect us, so she didn't tell us she put herself on the list? Okay, and I got a 5.0 GPA," Willow teased.

Calmer, Pia said, "I don't know what her rationale was. I left with you guys and didn't hear her out. All I'm saying is, we've all had situations where we needed people to listen to our side. People at the school hate me right now because three guys got carted off in handcuffs, but they raped me, okay? And if people would hear my story and understand what I went through, they'd get off my back. But because they're assuming, they're all over my tail. It's wrong for people to not get all the facts before they outcast somebody. I just thought our

67

friendship was deeper than that, that's all I'm saying. The fact is that all of us haven't been in Octavia's shoes. No, we didn't put ourselves on the list, but we've been in situations where we had to respond in ways other people didn't approve of to survive or to get our point across. I just think all of a sudden we're all high and mighty and think we're better than her. And that is really not a friendship I want to be a part of. To think we're better than her and can't hear her out is just the oddest."

CHAPTER ELEVEN
Purest (Sanaa's Ending)

Ms. Davis was holding the last swoop list counseling session of the year for the girls. Reluctantly, Sanaa attended. There was no love between all of them right now. They didn't all hate each other, but Sanaa just felt their lovey-dovey bond had always been too good to be true anyway. They'd all be graduating soon and going in their own directions to start their lives, so why try to fix things now? To Sanaa, this plan seemed like the best way not to get her feelings hurt. So she let everyone else do some of the talking in the session with Ms. Davis.

"Do you all know where Octavia is?" Ms. Davis asked.

"We're not her keeper," Willow uttered under her breath.

"So everything I said went in one ear and out the other?" Pia questioned. "You need to listen."

"I know you ain't tryna tell me what to do," Willow said.

Pia snapped back, "Somebody needs to tell you because your big head only thinks you're right."

"Okay, girls, settle down," Ms. Davis said. "What has gotten into you ladies? You were inseparable at the prom. Now you're at each other's throats."

"What does it matter anyway? We're all about to graduate! Who cares if we're not friends anymore?" Sanaa finally yelled out, letting them know how she truly felt.

"There it is. Our little friendship was fake all along," Willow said. "I knew it. Nobody really cares for anybody else anymore."

"I care," Olive said.

"And I care too," Pia uttered.

"And you know you care too," Ms. Davis said to Willow. "Sanaa, so do you. I don't need to know all the details of the rift going on between you guys, but I will say forgiveness is in order when it comes to having friendships. Being in any relationship, you got to have forgiveness. If you don't let things go, and you think you can survive on your own, you'll do things and say things that you don't mean and that you can't take back. You need to have a support group around you. You need to treat others the way you'd like to be treated. Sanaa, you're right. You guys will be going in different directions, but now is the training ground. You begin to learn life lessons in high school. You must decide which road you want to set yourself up for. The road that will be one of happiness, caring, forgiveness, and love, or one that is bitter, dark, and depressing."

"Why do you care and give so much to us?" Sanaa asked Ms. Davis.

Olive added, "Yeah, it's deeper than your job. I know it. I feel it."

"So just accept it," Ms. Davis said. "And

don't make me feel like my time was in vain. I'm sure Octavia is hurting, as are you guys. If you harbor bitterness, you can't be a true leader; you can't be really happy when you have hate within your heart. Now go on to class, unless you need to talk to me one on one."

Sanaa was the first to get up. She knew there was a lot she wanted to get right with life. She did want to choose the path that led to happiness, but how could she fix everything that was wrong? Out in the hallway, Sanaa saw Toni walking her way, but what could she say to a girl she'd betrayed? A girl she tried to fix things with. A girl she knew hated her so much that she messed up her car. Sanaa thought their relationship was absolutely irreconcilable. But Toni was smiling.

"Urgh, I can't believe this girl," Sanaa said to herself in a low voice. "She's walking the halls with a big old smile on her face. She wants to rub it in that she tore up my property and I let her get away with it. Oh my gosh, she's boasting."

"Can I talk to you for a second?" Toni surprised Sanaa by saying as they passed each other.

"I guess," Sanaa responded, even though she was very skeptical.

"I wanted to give you this twenty dollars." Toni handed the cash over to Sanaa.

"For what?"

"I had no right damaging your property. And I don't know how to ask you to forgive me without me paying for it."

"You are paying for the damage?"

Toni nodded. "Yeah, that should cover the cost of getting your car washed. But let me know if it costs more. I was stupid. I was angry."

"No, you were justified. You sent me to talk to Miles a long time ago, and I never told you I liked him too."

"I knew he liked you, and I knew you liked him too. Yet I sent you to do the impossible. I didn't know you'd keep it from me, so when I found out, I was angry. Now I need your forgiveness for putting you on the swoop list."

Sanaa raised her eyebrows. "So you did turn my name in?"

"I'm sure you figured it out already."

"I had a big hunch, but for a while I thought Miles did it."

"No, he's always cared for you and only you. I tried to get with him many times. I probably liked him because I knew you did. I don't know. I've been jealous of you for so long."

"I been jealous of you too," Sanaa admitted. "You can eat anything and not gain a pound."

"What kind of friendship did we really have?" Toni asked.

"Not a very good one."

"But I did love you," Toni sincerely shared. "I wanted to be like you, even though it was warped and messed up how I acted it all out. There's a lot of admiration I still feel in my heart for you, Sanaa."

"Ditto, girl. But you know it's gonna be hard to repair our friendship."

"I've missed being your friend, though. And, I knew I needed to be honest with you if I ever wanted a chance to be your friend again. We're about to go to college. So I'm not sure we'll able to restart our friendship, but—" Toni dropped her head in dejection.

Sanaa lifted her chin and said, "Yes, we can always start again."

"You got your swoop list girls now. You don't need me."

"What you're saying isn't true. Like I said, keeping it real, rebuilding the trust won't be easy for either of us, but I want us to try."

They hugged really tight. In the embrace, Sanaa felt the love and genuineness they shared. They agreed to talk more later on. When Sanaa walked on to class, she felt so excited that she and Toni had a big breakthrough with a conversation that was the purest.

CHAPTER TWELVE

Sweetest (Willow's Ending)

Willow had heard all the forgiveness talk, and she was fine that it wasn't sinking into her heart. In her mind, sometimes people needed to be cut off. If you're too nice, then people walk all over you, she thought. The dance team was having tryouts for the next year, and Willow was going to make it a point to be there and confront Hillary. What Willow hadn't faced was the fact that if Hillary had started the list, then Hillary was probably the one who put her name on it. Willow didn't have to psych herself up for what she was going to say.

Willow was ready to rip a new one into

Hillary, but she wasn't prepared to see her nemesis balled up in a corner, crying. As mad as Willow was at Hillary, seeing her in a somber state made Willow have compassion.

"What's wrong?" Willow uttered, not wanting to be too nice.

Hillary looked up and said, "Oh, just my luck you'd see me at the moment I found out my world was over."

"What do you mean, Hillary? Your world is over? You are always on top of the world."

"Joke's on me this time, Willow. As much as I've done to try and pull you down, looks like I should have been paying attention to my own life."

"What are you talking about?"

"I'm not going to graduate, okay!" Hillary huffed.

"Huh?" Willow was dumbfounded. She knew Hillary wasn't a brain, but to not graduate? "Really? Is this a joke?"

"You're looking at me like I don't know the letter I just got," Hillary replied in an upset tone. "My mom's already planned a big celebration.

We've got family and friends coming to see me walk, and I'm not going to march, alright? That's what I get, though. Starting the swoop list, it all comes back on me. What am I gonna do? How am I gonna face everybody? I wanted you to have nothing. Now I'm the one who's going to be looking stupid."

Willow couldn't believe what she was hearing. Hillary was remorseful. But there was one question Willow wanted answered.

Willow asked, "Why did you hate me so much?"

"When it came to you, I was always on the wrong side of everything. Eleventh-grade attendant on the homecoming court, you got it. Lead dancer, you got it. And Dawson, you got it," Hillary explained.

"But when the list came out, he and I weren't even together," Willow uttered as she scratched her head.

Hillary shook her head and grunted. "You don't even remember. Back in the fall, I was trying to talk to him, and you laughed in my face and sashayed off with him. I thought if he knew you were a tramp, he'd want me."

"Funny, Dawson always knew I needed to cool down, but he liked me anyway," Willow said, having her own revelation.

"I know that now. Me creating the list stopped you from messing around with so many guys and sent you into his arms. I'm sorry I put you on the list, and I'm sorry I created the list."

"Honestly, you did me a favor."

Hillary smiled and said, "Good, but I'm also sorry I was dogging Pia. Those boys raped several other girls."

"Are you serious?" Willow asked.

"Yep, that's what's coming out. I defended their butts."

"You didn't know," Willow said, even as she couldn't believe she was being so nice to Hillary. But she saw no fun in kicking a girl when she was down.

Being on the swoop list, she'd been the victim and felt people's verbal attacks and constant badgering. And while things had gotten a lot better, she still felt the pain and didn't want to make anyone else feel as low. Even if that person happened to be the one who caused her all the grief in the first place.

Willow sat down beside Hillary, pulled out the tissues from her purse, gave one to Hillary, and said, "Look, so you're gonna have to repeat a couple classes. Might not be the way you want it to go, but it's not the end of the world. Better learn a lesson that we shouldn't chase popularity and drama when we need to be chasing our dreams and our education. This little hiccup will propel you to greatness. Now you've learned a lesson, so when you get in somebody's college, you're gonna be focused."

"Get in somebody's college? I'm not even getting a high school degree. Give me a break."

"You're not getting a degree next week. But that doesn't mean you're not gonna get one by the end of the summer."

"But then I would have missed my opportunity to go to college."

"So, maybe you wait one year or one semester. Or, maybe you go to a two-year school and get your grades up. You can actually save some money that way."

"What do you mean?"

"Right now you won't be qualified for the Hope Scholarship. But if you go to a great place like Georgia Perimeter Community College, take your basic classes, and get at least get a 3.0, then you can transfer. And you will qualify for the Hope Scholarship and will have saved a bunch of money. Lots of community colleges are more affordable but offer the same basic classes with teachers who care."

"And how do you know?"

"I've heard people talk about it at my mom's church. Lots of kids go that route. She was thinking about it for me, but I'm gonna go ahead and go to Spelman."

"Oh my gosh! You're going to Spelman? I'm going nowhere!"

"Hillary, what are you talking about? My life is not your life. That has been your problem. Stay in your lane. Don't worry about mine."

Hillary sighed. "You're right."

Willow stayed there and joked with Hillary for another few minutes until Hillary went from crying to laughing. Willow didn't want to be her best friend, but she didn't want to leave her somber either.

"You taught me something," Willow said to Hillary before they parted.

"What? How 'what goes around, comes around' is the truth?"

"No. If I can have empathy for you while you're going through this, then I'm not the big, mean, bad wolf after all. That's good to know."

Hillary called for a truce, thanked Willow for her support, and said, "Yeah, deep down I must admit, between the two of us, you're the sweetest."

CHAPTER THIRTEEN
Bravest (Olive's Ending)

Olive was moved as she left the baccalaureate service that kicked off the week of graduation. It was the first time she got to pose for pictures in her own cap and gown. It was the first time she marched in with her class. The graduation ceremony wasn't until the end of the week, but already she felt special.

The most memorable part of it all for Olive was hearing a speech from Ms. Sealy, teacher of the year. She charged the students to be the star in their own lives. The meat of the message was to strive for excellence, to be tough and enduring, to have an attitude that's always positive, and to radiate light wherever their feet may tread.

Things were still a little tense in the foster home between Olive and Charles. It wasn't as bad as before. They were speaking. They knew they cared about each other. Things weren't the best either, though.

If Olive wanted to be the star in her own life, she decided, she might as well start then and there. She had to put her conflict with Tiger away for good. So, when she saw Tiger in the hallway, looking at her like he wanted to devour her for dinner, she walked up to him. He was all smiles. She was serious.

"We need to talk," she told him.

"Yeah, beautiful, we do."

She looked at all of his cronies hanging around him and said, "Can we talk alone?"

Tiger gave his boys a dismissive glare, and they all scattered. To Olive's surprise, before should could speak, Tiger straightened up. Suddenly, he wasn't so ghetto and cool. He acted like he had some sense. In a gentleman's voice, he declared, "I owe you an apology."

"Huh?" Olive was thwarted from her agenda of telling him off.

"Yeah, your boy can clean up. Don't get it twisted. I can still take down anybody I want, but I had some of my police friends shed some light on a brother. I'm going to try to clean myself up. I know if I want good karma, I need to set things right with you."

"I'm listening."

"I just wanted to control you. I just wanted you to want to be with me. I've always known that Charles dude liked you. Every time I'd come around the house and pick you up or walk with you in school, he'd look at me like he wanted to take me down. He got under my skin. One time I saw you talking to him—this was way before we broke up—and I thought you didn't like me anymore, or I thought you were playing me. So I tried to distance myself. And that's when I asked you to hook up with my boys. I wanted to hurt you like you hurt me."

"But you told me to get with those boys."

"I know I told you to, but I didn't think

you would be that stupid or have such low self-esteem that you'd do it."

This was really hard for Olive to hear because Tiger was being frank. Why was she so frail that when he asked her to do something appalling, she had complied? Back then, she hadn't wanted to lose him. She'd thought that if she didn't do what he wanted, she would. But, ultimately, she ended up losing him anyway, as well as her pride.

Tiger went on, "But I still felt angry toward you. So, I put your name on the swoop list and then I broke up with you."

Olive felt her stomach turn. Inside, she'd always worried that Charles was right, that Tiger had put her name on the list. But she'd never wanted to believe it.

Tiger looked at her and said, "Listen. I was wrong for tricking you that way, playing with you, and belittling you, when, to me, you've always been precious. When I put you on that list, as weird as it may seem, I ended up setting you free. I thought you were going to need me more after that. Actually, it turned you into the girl I've always known was inside. So really, you should thank me."

"Oh, I should, huh?" Olive said as she sort of smiled.

Tiger smiled. But when Olive saw Charles approaching, she put out both of her hands, one in front of Tiger's chest and one toward Charles's.

"Okay, guys, we're not going to do any of that. We're on church grounds. It's time to call a truce."

Tiger stepped up and said, "No, it ain't going to be none of that. I told him I wanted to talk to him, too."

Olive looked at Charles. "Huh?"

Tiger extended his hand to Charles, and Olive stepped out of the way.

"You're a much better man for her than me. Take care of my girl. You got mad balls for standing up to me. I need to concede that you're the right one for her."

"You told her you put her on the list?" Charles asked, probably wanting her to hear from Tiger what he had already known all along.

"Yeah, he told me. Can we have a moment?" she said to Charles.

He nodded, firmly shook Tiger's hand, and walked away.

"Are you going to stop gang banging?" Olive said to him.

"Aw, you still care about me."

"I should kick you in the groin. That's what I should do with all you put me through. But with what you just said, all that you admitted, and all that you conceded, all is forgiven."

"Well." He leaned over and gave her a kiss on the cheek. "I'm trying to work on me, but sometimes you're in too deep to get out. That's why I want you to stick with a guy like Charles and not me."

"It took guts to be real with me like that. The Tiger you've just shown me here, I know if he wanted to get out of the gang, he could. Of all the dudes I know, you're the bravest."

CHAPTER FOURTEEN
Sincerest (Octavia's Ending)

Coming out of the baccalaureate service, Octavia was hand in hand with Shawn. She sat with him during the program, but she kept looking over at her girls, wishing she was with them. It was so ironic because she was now back in the same position she was at the beginning of the school year. No crew wanted her to be around. While she was overjoyed things with Shawn were going right, seeing Sanaa, Willow, Olive, and Pia pose for pictures without her broke her heart.

Seeing her down, Shawn said, "You know, I can talk to Olive if you want me to. I know she cares about you. You asked me to leave it alone, so

89

I haven't gotten on her, but this ain't even cool."

"No, I don't wanna be around anybody who doesn't want me around them. Please don't talk to Olive and push the issue. If anything, I learned I gotta be happy with me. I need to be okay standing by myself."

"Oh, so if I walked away, you wouldn't be mad?" Shawn teased.

"Come on, Shawn, I'm serious. I wanted to be a part of a group so bad that I lied and turned myself into some freak girl just to get attention."

"Yeah, but it's more than that for you. I know you care about those girls."

She really appreciated Shawn because he was telling the truth. Her heart was big for her swoop list sisters. She kept up with their scoop online. She was happy that Sanaa had gotten things cleared up with Toni. She was overjoyed that Hillary had come clean to Willow and that Willow was there for her in her darkest hour. She was glad that Tiger had let Olive go completely, and she was deeply concerned about Pia, hoping that she would give Stephen a chance to explain why he betrayed her so. Because Octavia cared so much, it tore her up on the inside that the girls who meant so much to her didn't reciprocate her feelings. However, she knew she had no one else to blame but herself. She should've told them the truth long ago. Keeping it cost her so much.

"You think you could take a picture with us?" she heard a familiar voice say from behind.

Octavia dared not turn around. She looked at Shawn, and he was smiling. When she turned around, she couldn't believe it. All four of the swoop list girls were standing right there.

"Okay, what? You can't forgive us for being jerks?" Willow uttered as Octavia just rushed to her and gave her the biggest hug. "Alright, alright. Don't mess up the dress."

"Are you kidding? You guys want to take a picture with me? You're coming over here to talk to me? You wanna apologize to me? I owe you guys apologies!" Octavia explained.

"No, we owe you one," Sanaa said. "It took Pia to talk some sense into us. Who are we to judge? I hate that you had to feel so low to put yourself on this crazy list, but you weren't trying to hurt us in the process."

"Yep, it's not like you put any of us on it," Olive said.

"Besides, anybody that desperate for swoop friends," Willow joked, "deserves to keep misfits around."

"You're not misfits," Octavia said. "We're just a real bunch."

The girls all stared at Willow. Octavia didn't know what they wanted her to say. Willow sucked her lips.

"Okay, I also need to apologize for calling you a white heffa," Willow blurted out.

"No biggie, brown bully . . . I mean beauty," Octavia coughed and joked.

The girls giggled and made up. They all posed and took selfies. Octavia was delighted she had learned not to hide from her mistakes, but to learn from them. She understood that she needed to be strong, with or without friends. And that her true friends would came back to her because they loved her. That was a lesson she was never going to forget.

Pia asked Octavia if she'd go with her to the restroom.

Octavia was happy to comply. As they walked, she put her arm around Pia and said, "Thank you. Thank you for not letting them hate me."

Pia smiled and said, "Thank you for giving us another chance."

"You know, you probably need to do the same thing with Stephen. He's following us."

Pia quickly turned around and stopped dead in her tracks when she saw that Octavia was right. Pia huffed. Octavia wanted to help her girl make things right.

"You should at least hear him out!"

Pia boldly demanded, "Okay, but you're not going anywhere."

"What he has to say is private."

"You are not going anywhere!"

Stephen walked over to them. Octavia tried to slip away, but Pia wouldn't let her. Octavia stopped moving and stood by her girl.

"Whatever you have to say to me, you can say to the both of us."

Stephen said, "I wanted to tell you that I'm not ashamed I put you on the list."

"Excuse me?" Octavia said, not wanting to get in it but unable to help herself.

"Okay, now can we move on?" Pia said. "I knew he wasn't ashamed of what he did."

"If y'all would just listen!" Stephen called out.

"Okay, we're listening. Talk." Pia said.

"The guys, the night they raped you, they were bragging that they wanted to do it again. And they wanted to do it again to you because you were pure."

"But they'd just raped me. I wasn't pure any-more," Pia rationalized.

"To them you were still pure. They were the only guys to be with you. So when I saw a notice about the swoop list, I figured I'd put your name out there. When they saw you on it, they mostly backed away. I'm not saying I deserve a medal for what I did, but I was trying to protect you from them. Love me or hate me, my crazy tactic worked."

"His motives may be a little suspect," Octavia leaned over to Pia and said. "But forgive him, girl, 'cause your hot señor's intentions were the sincerest."

CHAPTER FIFTEEN
Best (Pia's Ending)

Sitting with her classmates at the graduation ceremony, Pia was overwhelmed. All was good between her and Stephen again. Her mom was still doing amazingly well. Finally, she was a high school graduate.

The ceremony was touching, but it went by fast. With so much of her life right, she was tripping when she looked around and saw many eyes looking her way. Over the course of the semester, one would have thought she would have been used to it. When she was placed on the swoop list, she was stared at and dissected. When the swoop list girls dressed up for the big basketball play-off game and brought a lot of attention to themselves, people had glared at and analyzed her. When three boys in her senior class were hauled away in handcuffs after she accused them of rape, she was looked at and scrutinized. As she threw up the hand that didn't hold her diploma, she wondered what in the heck was wrong now.

She rushed over to Ms. Davis, who was waving her down in excitedly. "You did it, Pia! You're a graduate, girl! Oh my gosh, I'm so proud of you!"

As Ms. Davis hugged her tight, she said, "Yeah, thanks, thanks, thanks, but why are all these people staring at me? What is it now?"

"Oh, Pia, it's nothing bad. Haven't you heard? You're a hero!"

"What are you talking about?"

"Two other girls in the school have come forward saying that they were also raped. One was blindfolded similar to your story, so she couldn't be sure it was those same guys. But the description and everything that happened was exactly like your experience. It was after a game one day. She was by herself, and they grabbed her. The other girl had a similar experience. One of the boys admitted to her that he'd done it. But she wasn't going to say anything because she thought it was her fault. Then, with you coming forward, it was a no-brainer for her to do the same thing."

Pia clutched her diploma over her heart. "Are you serious?"

"Yes, I am. And I'm so proud of you," Ms. Davis said. "Actually, the strength of all five of you girls makes me proud. I just wish my niece would have been able to hold on too."

"Your niece?"

"Nothing," Ms. Davis said, getting a little emotional.

As she walked away, Pia watched her wipe away tears and thought of the different times that Ms. Davis had given hints of not being able to help someone else or this infamous niece. Before she could put it all together, she was practically tackled by her girls.

"We graduated!" Willow said as she did a cool dance. Octavia and Sanaa tried to copy Willow's moves, but they were not as cool.

"Come on, Pia, help me out. These girls can't dance," Willow chuckled.

"Speak for them," Olive said as she busted a cool move.

Pia motioned for them to settle down. "No, guys, listen. I think I know who's been writing the Leah letters."

"Who?" Sanaa asked.

"I know it wasn't Hillary," Willow said. "She wasn't that caring."

"And for sure not Stephen or any of our guys," Olive uttered. "They weren't that sensitive."

"Tell us," Octavia begged, tugging on Pia's arm.

Pia took a deep breath. "I'm not sure, but I think it's Ms. Davis."

Willow looked betrayed. "What do you mean, Ms. Davis?"

Pia explained, "I think it's her. She mentioned a niece and not being able to save her or something."

"Well, let's go confront her." Willow huffed and uttered.

"What?" Pia said, trying to hold Willow back.

Willow jerked from Pia's grip and shouted, "Naw, she's been writing us these weird letters and been all close to us like she cares. Sending us eerie stuff from beyond the grave, scaring people half to death and junk. We need to get to the bottom of this. That stuff is not cool."

"I don't have any room to talk," Octavia added.

Olive nudged Octavia and said, "Yes you do! If she duped you, you need to know."

"Girls!" Ms. Davis excitedly said when they stood before her.

They all gave Pia a grueling stare, so reluctantly she said, "We have a question."

"Yeah, and please tell us the truth," Willow uttered with her usual big attitude as she placed her hand on her hip.

Still grinning, Ms. Davis said, "Sure. I'll answer anything."

Pia went in her phone and pulled up the last Leah note. "Did you send me this? Have you been the one writing the letters from Leah?"

Ms. Davis looked away. They could see a dejected look. The girls were dumbfounded by her reaction.

"Oh my gosh! You have been!" Willow screamed out.

"Just let her talk," Sanaa said.

"Yeah, please, let her explain," Octavia said to Willow.

Ms. Davis said, "Last year at this time, I was burying my niece. Her name was Leah Golf, and she went to a school in Warner Robbins. She was on the swoop list there. She was the only one on it at her school, and it was horrible."

"We know," Pia uttered.

"That's right!" Ms. Davis replied, "You guys went down there and visited. We talked about it."

"Yeah, but you didn't tell us that was your niece, nor did you tell us you were writing us the notes," Willow said.

Ms. Davis said, "I know I didn't, and I'm sorry. See, I couldn't help my niece, and every day I regret that I couldn't be there for her. However, I could be there for you guys. When

I saw the swoop list surface, I wanted do everything I could to help you all see that a dumb list that was devised to pull you down could be used to build you up. If you never forgive me, I understand. But with all my heart, I meant no harm."

Ms. Davis turned to walk away, but Pia grabbed her and hugged her tight. All the other four girls joined in. The emotion that all of them shared was overwhelming and real.

"We thank you," Pia said. "You've been there for us all along. And you're right, you helped us become better."

Sanaa chimed in, "We've learned to give it up—our foolish ways, that is."

Willow said, "Yeah, I'm always hard on you, but you showed us how to get on our knees and pray. We really need true faith in our lives."

Olive said, "And I liked it when you told us to back that thing up. We didn't have to be in a boy's face. We could go back in our lives and learn from our past mistakes."

"And to truly feel real good," Octavia shared, "was to give back to others."

Pia said, "And you told us that to be true leaders, if we want to sit on top, we've got to find forgiveness and help those who have hurt us."

"And y'all have done all those things. I believe Leah is smiling down. And I'm so proud of you," Ms. Davis said. "Now all of you are truly at your best."

ACKNOWLEDGMENTS

Sit on top . . . to achieve greatness you have to be willing to stay positive, remain dedicated, and help others! As I sit on the mountain of completion after finishing this book and series, I have to thank those who helped me rise.

To my parents, Dr. Franklin and Shirley Perry, sitting on top I am thankful you gave me vision. To my publisher, especially Lindsey Matvick, I am thankful for your unending help with publicity. To my extended family, I feel a sense of accomplishment because of your support. To my assistants Ashely Cheathum, Alyxandra Pinkston, and Candace Johnson, I am grateful because you all helped me get another great series done. To my dear friends, especially Gwen Tatum and Melissa Mims, I strive for excellence because I hear you cheering me on. To my teens, Dustyn, Sydni, and Sheldyn, it is bittersweet to watch you enter into the next phase of your lives. To my husband, Derrick, I'm thankful for you. To my readers, especially the kids in Jackson, GA, sitting on top I pray this bully swoop list disappears from all schools. And to my Father, another series done and not knowing what's next, I trust You.

ABOUT THE AUTHOR

STEPHANIE PERRY MOORE is the author of more than sixty young adult titles, including the Sharp Sisters series, the Grovehill Giants series, the Lockwood Lions series, the Payton Skky series, the Laurel Shadrach series, the Perry Skky Jr. series, the Yasmin Peace series, the Faith Thomas Novelzine series, the Carmen Browne series, the Morgan Love series, the Alec London series, and the Beta Gamma Pi series. Mrs. Moore is a motivational speaker who enjoys encouraging young people to achieve every attainable dream. She lives in the greater Atlanta area with her husband, Derrick, and their three children. Visit her website at www.stephanieperrymoore.com.

READ ALL THE BOOKS IN THE
SWOOP LIST SERIES:

THE **SHARP** SISTERS